BEWARE THE MIGHTY BITEY

written by

Heather Pindar

illustrated by

Susan Batori

For David, who is MIGHTY. – H.P.

To Robert, who makes me laugh every day even when I am grumpy. – S.B.

Deep in the jungle hung a
fraying, swaying rope bridge.

Gliding below, through the still waters of the Nippy Pool, watching, hoping, waiting, were...

CROOAAK!

...The Mighty Bitey Piranhas.

They were singing their favourite song:

"We are the Mighty Bitey,
BEWARE our raZor teeth!
Snick snack, click clack,
ZZZZZZZZZZZZ!"

"Shhhhhhh. Someone's coming,"
said Chief Bitey.

Scritch-scratch,
scritch-scratch.

Along came...

...Mouse.

"Where are you going, Mouse?"
called Chief Bitey.

"I'm off to play my ukulele
at Cougar's party."

"Oh please stay a moment, and play for us,"
wheedled Chief Bitey,
"Can you dance too? Oh do say yes."

"Really? You'd like to hear me play? With pleasure!" said Mouse.

So Mouse danced and played his ukulele:

The rope bridge **swayed** and **frayed** and **slipped** and **dipped** just a **little bit**.

The Mighty Bitey grinned and cried, "More! More!"

Tip-tappity,

tip-tappity,

tip-tappity tap-tap.

Along came...

...**Goat** with his steel drums.

"Please play for us!" called the Mighty Bitey.

"Okey-dokey," said Goat.

Ding-ding,
dung-dung,
ding dong **dung**,

went the drums.

The rickety rope bridge
swayed and **frayed**
and **slipped** and **dipped**
just a little bit **more**.

Thump! Thumpity-thump!

Along came...

...Bear with his tuba, on the way to Cougar's party.

"Give us a tune, Bear. Please," said Chief Bitey.

"If you like," said Bear. So he did...

Roompah, roompah, oom-papah!

The rope bridge
swayed and **frayed** and
slipped and **dipped** a little bit **too much.**
The Mighty Bitey Piranhas' grins got even bigger.

SNAP!

Down slipped the rope bridge.

It hung by a single twisting twine.

All was still, except...

...a butterfly, which fluttered in the breeze, soft and silent as a snowflake,

left...right...up a bit...

down a bit...

OOPS

and landed delicately on the **slipping, dipping** rope bridge.

Everyone held their breath.
C r e a k ...

SNAP! SNAP!

SNAP!

CRASH!

The bridge tore away from the canyon walls.

"Zzzzzzzzzzzz!" grinned Chief Bitey. "Here comes lunch!"

DOWN

DOWN

DOWN

tumbled Mouse, Goat and Bear
and fell with a great big...

OUT swooshed the water.

UP Flew the Mighty Bitey Piranhas THEN...

Goat's steel drums

and Bear's tuba.

"Mmmm, yum yum!" said Bear.

Beware the Mighty Bitey
An original concept by author Heather Pindar
© Heather Pindar
Illustrated by Susan Batori

MAVERICK ARTS PUBLISHING LTD
Studio 3A, City Business Centre, 6 Brighton Road, Horsham,
West Sussex, RH13 5BB, +44 (0)1403 256941
© Maverick Arts Publishing Limited November 2017
Published November 2017

A CIP catalogue record for this book
is available at the British Library.

ISBN 978-1-84886-284-5

Maverick
arts publishing

www.maverickbooks.co.uk